This book belongs to

....

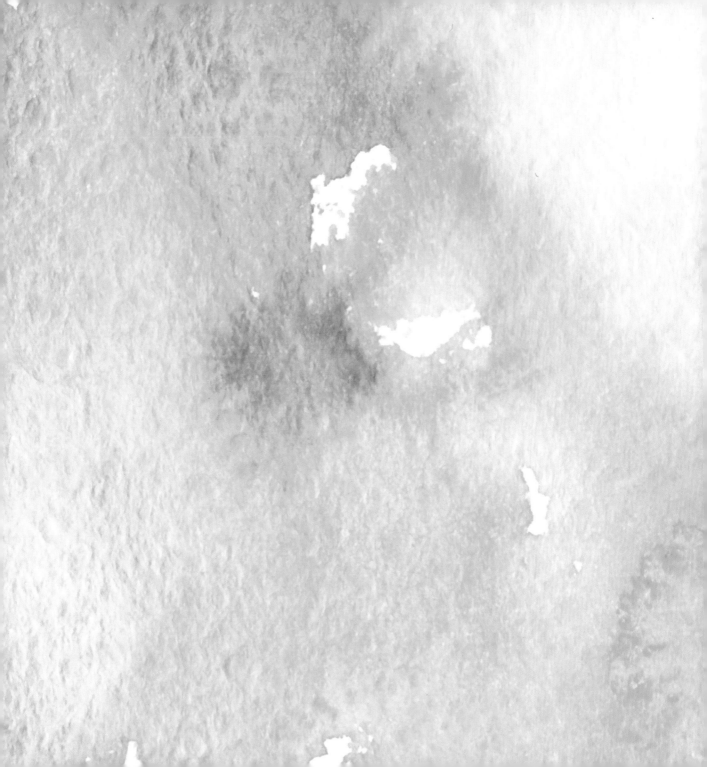

Copyright © 2021
make believe ideas ltd

The Wilderness, Berkhamsted, Hertfordshire, HP4 2AZ, UK.
557 Broadway, New York, NY 10012, USA.

www.makebelieveideas.com

Illustrated by Nadine Wickenden.

Love is the Greatest!

Nadine Wickenden

make
believe
ideas

Love is **very** patient
and kind.

It doesn't want what belongs to others.

It *isn't* rude.
It *doesn't* think about *itself*.

Love doesn't get **upset** with **others**.

It doesn't keep track of wrongs.

when **others** do **wrong.**

Love **never** gives up on people.

Love **never** stops trusting.

Love *never* loses hope,

and *never quits.*

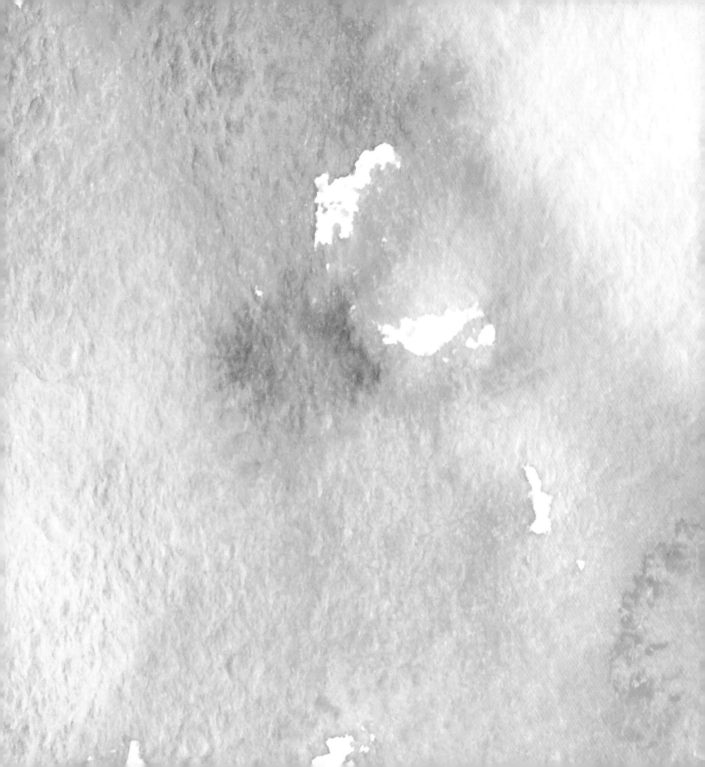